Is There More?
A Short Story Collection:
By:
BRITTNEY RZ.

Featuring "Whole Again," an Honorable Mention in Writer Digest's 84th Annual Writing Competition.

Edited by: Elizabeth Buege

Cover design by: Kelly Lipovich

ISBN-10:0692541284
ISBN-13:978-0-692-54128-9

CONTENTS

Dedication.
For my parents who always believe in me. This book would never have gotten here without the both of you!

A FEW WORDS FROM ME:

One of my favorite ways to explore ideas for stories is to ask the question, What if? What if books could talk to you? What if you could reset a human to the last time everything worked properly like you can with a computer? What if you were handed a "Choose your own adventure," novel that mapped out your life for you? What would the consequences be of these ideas? Where could the lives of the characters living through these situations end up?

I remember when I was young I was in the Power of the Pen competition with my school. Our teacher told you us during practice that the way to get the judges attention was to take the prompt and run far and wide with it. That is advice I have carried with me for my entire writing life. I always try to come up with an idea, map out the traditional ways to answer a question or think of an idea and then go in the complete opposite direction.

I want nothing more than for my readers to finish each story wondering what else is possible. Where else could the characters have gone or be going? I have always loved stories that leave bits and pieces up in the air allowing me as the reader to continue the story in my own mind.

I want you to read each of these stories and to see the number of possibilities that surround our everyday lives. Each one of these tales are set in our modern day world, the surroundings feel comfortable and familiar. I want you to sink in and to think about what else could be out there. What else is possible if we just open our minds and consider all the possibilities around us.

As you read always be asking yourself is there more? Is there more to these stories? Is there more to the world that surrounds us? Is there more to the lives that we all live?

ALWAYS BEEN OURS

"YOU'VE BEEN HOLDING out on me," Kiera said as she swallowed the last savory bite of the meal. She wiped her mouth and placed the napkin beside her plate.

"You've never let me near the stove," James replied as he pulled the empty plates toward himself.

"That's because you burn Pop Tarts. I was supposed to trust you with an oven? Really?" Kiera stacked the silverware on top of the plates.

"Well, I made the meal, which means you get the dishes." He stood up and placed the stack in the sink grinning at her.

She scowled at him. "Another reason I do the cooking. I hate dishes." She jutted out her lower lip at him, trying to get some sympathy.

"Good try. I'll hold the movie until you're done." He kissed her forehead and left for the living room.

"Damn," she huffed as he left the room. She knew she should just get up and get the whole ordeal over with. Instead, she tipped her chair back onto two legs, hands holding tight onto the table to keep herself from falling over backwards. She leaned her head over the back of the chair and stared at the full sink. Nope. Even upside down, they still looked like a mess she didn't want to go near.

"Wash yourselves," she muttered at them. They didn't move. She groaned. If she had superpowers, she determined, she would just use them so she could be super lazy. She stared at a fork, throwing all she had into trying to get it to flinch even a tiny bit. Still nothing. She was just about to actually get up when everything around her went completely silent.

The whir of the fridge and the murmured voices from the television were all gone. It was as if someone had hit mute on the world. Complete and impenetrable silence surrounded her. She let the chair legs fall to the ground, but no loud thud greeted her ears. Her finger went into her ear, and she was desperately turning it around and around, trying to find whatever had caused the world to go so quiet, when she heard a low, consistent hiss. It sounded like the small snakes that sometimes snuck up on her in the garden.

Her legs shot up off the ground, and she wrapped her arms around her knees. Her eyes scanned the ground, desperately searching for the slithering little creature. She saw nothing.

A second later, the bubble of silence that had fallen over the kitchen popped, and the living sounds of the house rushed back to her ears. The TV was loud, with shouting and cries. Birds chirped and the wind whistled in the trees outside the window. There were hurried footsteps coming down the hallway.

"Hey, I said, 'Are you alright?' I heard a bang." James stood in the doorway. She knew he had to be slightly confused as he took in the scene before him. She was curled up in her chair, eyes frantically scanning the ground over and over again.

"Huh? Yeah, fine. I was leaning back on my chair and got off balance. I fell forward," she told him, her voice low, never directly looking at him.

"Are you sure?" he asked. She heard his feet shuffle over the carpet and onto the kitchen tiles. She gave him the smallest shake of her head. He wanted to come to her side and wrap her in his arms, attempting to calm her down. She didn't need that, it had been nothing. Just a weird noise created by her tired brain, there was no need to draw out the incident.

"Yeah." Kiera gave him tightlipped grin as she slid her feet back onto the ground and stood up. Whatever had happened had to be from leaning her head backwards over the chair. It was probably a result of the blood rushing to her head or something.

"Give me fifteen minutes." She moved a pile of books away from the edge of the sink and placed them near the back of the counter. She mentally reminded herself to put them back in their places later.

Kiera filled the sink with warm water, added a generous amount of soap, and piled the dishes in the water. Thankfully, pasta had few dishes.

4

She was just putting a plate into the drying rack when the hairs on the back of her neck went up. The sound was back. The world did not go silent this time; everything just softened. The hissing was a few decibels louder. She gripped the edge of the sink, trying with all she had not to look around.

If she turned and saw a small slithering body making its way across the floor, she would break. James would come in, yelling and asking what was wrong. She would point at the devilish creature and his panic would fade into annoyance. He would remove the snake and she would have to listen to him tease her for weeks on end about the whole thing. She just closed her eyes and prayed it would go away, that it would find a hole to disappear into or go back to the outdoors where it belonged.

A minute later, the world was back to full volume once more. The hissing was gone. She cautiously glanced down at her feet. There was nothing there. She checked behind her. Nothing. She let out a deep held breath and went back to the task at hand.

As she quickly finished the last few items, she decided that she and James needed to have a serious conversation about moving to a city. This country living, with all of its creepy crawly creatures, would be the death of her.

Some paranormal investigations show was just ending as she made her way into the living room. James was laid out across the whole couch. She picked up his feet and sat in the corner. She propped her feet up on a pile of hardcover books on the coffee table. James let his feet fall back into her lap.

"Took you long enough," he said as he switched from the TV to the blue-ray player where the movie was queued up and ready to go.

"Quiet," she commanded, giving him a scowl. He laughed as he hit play.

Just as the piano began to swell and the title card came into focus, she heard one whispered word in her right ear. *Kiera.*

Her feet slipped off the books, causing a few to fall to the ground. Their pages splayed out, and covers bent backwards. She didn't bend down to fix the mess.

"What?" She scanned the empty air to her right from the ceiling to the floor.

"Huh?" James had paused the movie. "You okay?" he asked slowly.

"Did you hear that?" She looked over at him. His confused expression answered her question.

"Hear what?" He sat up.

"Someone whispered my name." She looked away, taking in the entire room. She saw a chair that had a thin layer of cat hair on it. Glanced at the flat carpet that was no more cushioned than a hardwood floor. A pile of blankets sat in the corner by the front door, the weather too hot for them at the moment. In front of her was just the coffee table, holding only one book now that the rest were scattered all over the floor. The black box TV was paused, a man standing with a hand straight out in front of him, palm up. No one else was in the room besides her and James.

He gave her a playful grin, one she didn't return. She knew she had heard something say her name. Yes, she was tired and yes, the last few months had been the most stressful of her life, but she was not losing it. She saw James arm twitch, as if to reach out for her. She moved to her right a few inches.

"Want to go to bed?" James asked, voice no longer joking but concerned.

"I'm fine." She hadn't meant to sound so harsh but her nerves were on edge and his picking and questioning was only making the whole thing worse. He gave her one more concerned look, before he restarted the movie.

Kiera concentrated completely on the words and cheesy music coming from the over-the-top romantic comedy playing on the screen. She listened to every word, focusing on each syllable. She focused on each note of the music. She looked only at the bright colors and moving figures inside the TV's frame. She was desperate to let her world be completely filled by the movie before her.

The movie passed in a blur, there were only ten minutes left. The romantic leads were confessing their undying love and apologizing for being so obtuse and stupid. The big reunion kiss was just about to happen when the voice came back.

"Come to us." It was still low, but the tone was harder, more commanding this time.

Kiera couldn't remember getting to her feet or walking down the hallway. A small part of her was screaming, *"What are you doing?"* but she ignored that part. James's desperate calls were only echoes in her ears. One foot slid in front of the other.

She reached the office, and her hand reached out and grasped the cool knob.

James's hands grabbed her upper arms and spun her around. She saw him before her, but he was hazy, out of focus. He was talking.

"Kiera, can you hear me? What are you doing?" She saw his lips moving, barely able to hear his words. His voice was so far away, as if he were talking to her from the top of a well while she was at the very bottom.

She stood up on her tiptoes and kissed his cheek. She didn't know why she did it, but it felt right.

She turned back to her office, opened the door, went inside, and shut the door in her concerned boyfriend's face. She locked it and went into the middle of the room. She felt her trance-like-state fall away for a moment, confusion and panic starting to seep in.

"Finally." This voice was different from the one that had been speaking to her before. It was the whispered whine of a teenage boy.

"Hush." This one came from directly in front her. It was soothing, like a kindly grandmother.

"Kiera, we have been waiting for you." This was the one from earlier. It was tough and cold. The tone conjured up the image of a no-frills businessman in a dark, crisp suit.

Who had been waiting for her? What did that mean? What was she doing standing here just talking to the air?

"For me?" she asked. She searched the room for who was speaking. All she saw was her ramshackle desk; paper, pens, and empty candy wrappers covered the surface.

The only other things in the room were four tall floor-to-ceiling bookshelves stuffed to bursting. Some of the books were brand-new, spines never creased. Others were so well-read that their covers were falling apart, and their pages were loose, hanging on for dear life.

Brittney RZ.

"What do you mean waiting?" She needed to keep the voices talking to keep herself from completely falling into a panicked mess. She scanned the room desperately looking for the hidden camera or speaker. Was this some terrible practical joke? She shook her head. It couldn't be, James was not this creative.

"You used to love us. We were your friends. Now we are covered in only dust, just forgotten tomes of the past," the teenager said.

She heard his words as she stared at the bookshelf directly in front of her. The realization was like a punch to her gut. Forgotten tomes? Used to love them? It was the books! Her books were whispering to her. She closed her eyes picturing the night. She saw them in a pile on the kitchen counter. In the living room, she had used them as a footrest before throwing them all over the floor. They had been surrounding her all night.

"I haven't forgotten you," she felt the words tumble from her lips. "I love you." She could barely say the sentence without a giggle. What was she talking about? She was lying through her teeth. They were right, she had let them become decoration more than anything else over the last year.

"Where do you go when your pen stops writing? To our pages and our stories? No, you go to that cursed black box with moving pictures or that silver machine with the world inside. We are just footrests now. Forgotten things on the counter." The grandmother no longer sounded sweet and kind. She was angry now, reprimanding.

"Sorry?" Kiera knew the words were empty, just a desperate rambling response. She did love her books, that was something that would never change. It was just the last year had been the most confusing and stressful of her life. She didn't have the time or patience to get involved in a story; one that would just give her yet another excuse to ignore her responsibilities. She could not afford to disappear into their stories right now. The television and internet let her turn her brain off and become nothing but a shell, no worries with no thinking. Two things she desperately needed in her life at the moment. Time to read was the one thing she missed most about her old life, but that was her past. She couldn't go back.

"'Sorry' is such an empty word," the man said.

"What can I do?" she asked. She knew she could promise to read

8

more, but she felt like that wasn't going to be enough for these voices. She also knew it would be an empty promise.

"Kiera!" She jumped. James was pounding on the door. How long had he been trying to get into the room? How long had she been standing there talking to the empty air?

"We have to hurry," the grandmother said.

"There is nothing you can do now," the man explained. "We are tired of waiting on you. You are ours—always have been. We made you. We molded how you think, how you see the world and how you interact with those around you. We did all the work of creating you. We tried to let you appreciate us, to use us to create new stories and lives so that we could continue our work. But you failed us. Now we will take you."

"Take me?" Her voice came out as a scared squeak. The concept terrified her but a piece of her understood what he meant. He had a point, without the stories in those pages she would not be the person she was now, for better or worse.

She tried to move forward, tried to run to the door, to James and freedom. But her feet were stuck firmly in place. She tried to lunge forward, but it was pointless. She couldn't move a single muscle.

The air around her became charged, and the hair on her arms stood up. The floor was drifting from side to side, the walls nothing but fuzzy outlines. She felt as if she was about to pass out.

She swayed on her feet, looking around for a way to get out. There had to be an escape. Her surroundings were starting to sparkle. Black and silver sparkles were covering everything. She looked down at her feet, and her heart stopped.

Where her foot had once been were only words now. The word "foot" just repeated over and over again, put together into the shape of the thing that had once allowed her to walk. As she watched, her right foot began to disintegrate into letters, as well.

Flesh flaked off, forming the letters, which then came together to form the word and fall into the place where there once had been bone and skin. The affliction crawled up her legs. Skin and bone were dissolving and reshaping into letters and words that were the very basic essence of who she was.

A tear slid down her cheek as she watched the transformation. How had it all come to this? She had once heard that the death of the author came when she no longer respected the stories that had spoken to and guided her, and she now knew how true that statement was.

This was all her fault. Instead of fear or anger, though, she suddenly felt relieved. For so long, she had been fighting to find her voice, to put the right words in order to say the right statements. In order to become someone the world wanted and approved of. Now, none of that mattered. Soon she would be those words and those ideas. As she felt her face contract and reform, she smiled. For so long, she had felt lost, constantly trying to find a place to hold onto. She had constantly been fighting against the tug of war inside of her. Now she was done searching and done fighting.

Sitting in front of the disaster of a desk was a book of short stories. It fluttered its pages and flew up into the air, consuming each and every word, thought, and idea that had once been Kiera. Once it was filled, it fell to the ground. When James was finally able to get inside the room, all he found lying in the center of the room was the book of short stories, sitting there still and silent.

So Many Faces

DEAR SOMEONE,

I don't know who you are. You could be a beautiful princess from a far-off land or from a planet we haven't even discovered yet. Or you could be a serial killer, and I am handing you a piece of paper that will be the end of me. To tell you the truth, I DO NOT CARE!!

I don't care who you are. I don't care where you are from, what you do, or what you look like. I just care that I love you. I love every single thing about you.

I love that we are best friends. I love that we can just watch a movie without saying a word, the silence being more than enough. I love that we can scream at each other one minute and be making out the next. I love that you think I hung the moon even though I have no idea where the step ladder is. I love that you make me feel special and happy. You make me feel safe and warm.

I love that..."

"I've been looking all over for you. What are you doing in here?" My roommate's voice startled me, and I dropped my pen. "Come on, we are next up in Beer Pong."

"Okay," I said, laying a hand over the paper. My roommate wasn't known for understanding the concept of privacy and personal space. He looked at me and down at the paper and came over to the desk. He shoved my hand off the paper and quickly grabbed the sheet. I tried to pull it back, but he was too quick.

He scanned the pages, his smile getting bigger and bigger. By the end, he was laughing so hard he could barely breathe, and tears were falling down his cheeks.

"How drunk are you? Please say more drunk then you have ever been before. Don't tell me you wrote this junk sober?" He wiped his eyes with the back of his hand. "Maybe I should find myself a new partner for the game. Looks like you're busy daydreaming over here."

"Fuck off," I snapped. "I'm buzzed, and it's for class." I grabbed the paper back from him. "It's due in the morning, and I forgot about it." I hoped he would buy my excuse. I shoved the paper into the top drawer.

"Sure it is. But you know, once I have a drink or two more, everyone will hear that mess." He flung an arm around my shoulders. "It's inevitable."

"Then it's also inevitable that you're going to end this night with a black eye." I told him, shrugging off his arm. He shoved me and headed out into the hallway.

I followed and shut off the light. I sighed as I took one more look at the shadow that was the desk that held my pathetic desperate scribblings. I headed down the hallway to find another beer.

****

I pulled open the drawer of my desk. It wasn't anything impressive, just plain cherry wood with two small drawers, but it was mine, and that was all that mattered. Only mine.

Smiling ear to ear, I examined my fresh, new space. I pulled open the bottom drawer - completely empty, just waiting for me to fill it. I closed the bottom drawer and opened the top drawer, also empty and waiting.

I took a deep breath and felt my heart lift as I took in all the potential that sat before me. I started to shut the drawer when something caught my eye. There was a piece of paper hanging onto the back of the drawer. I slid my hand in and twisted the sheet carefully until it came out. It was slightly yellowed, but not that old. It most likely belonged to the young man who had sold me the desk.

I spread it out and read it. It was a love letter to someone, someone he clearly didn't know yet. I laughed as I read it. The boy was so naive, so caught up in a romantic notion of love and life. How disappointed he would be when the world hit him, and it would hit him hard. Tears would fall when he realized that this was nothing but a writer's fantasy.

I got up and went to my bag hanging on the door. I fished around for a moment before I found a pen. I clicked it and sat back in front of the paper. This cute letter needed to be sliced up with a bit of reality.

I love that....you know what, scratch that. I don't love how you lied to me that night. You said you would be home, promised I wouldn't endure that rejection alone. You lied.

I don't love that when I confronted you, you told me to settle down. You said that I can't always rely on you and needed to learn that now.

I don't love how you yelled at me for crying that night. I lost my dream job, and you weren't there to hold me like you should have been. You told me to get a backbone and stop acting like such a little girl. I don't love how small you made me feel that night.

I don't love how you made me see the light. I know I needed the push, but not how you did it. You showed me I can't rely on anyone but myself. I don't love how much that hurt.

But I do love how strong I am now."

I put my pen down, a smile playing across my lips. That was what love truly was; a useless notion, full of hurt and empty words. Love ended with nothing but a crack in the heart and tears on the cheeks.

"Idiot," I laughed as I slid the paper through the crack in the drawer. I walked into the kitchen to make dinner.

****

13

Brittney RZ.

"This drawer is frickin' stuck," my girlfriend shouted from the bedroom.

"Is it a real drawer?" I called back from the living room, where I was busy trying to determine where to put the next picture.

"What?" she barked. "What kind of dumbass question is that?"

"Ugh." I put down the hammer and nails, hoping the cat wouldn't step on them.

I entered the room to find her sitting cross-legged on the floor, tugging and swearing at the desk. I wanted to just watch and let her try a few more choice words first. Inanimate objects responded to shouted curses and anger, right? But we had a house to decorate and a bed to break in, so I knew I had to help her.

"Sometimes, there are faux drawers for a purely aesthetic feel, nothing more," I said, standing behind her.

"That's dumb." She looked up at me. "The top one is real; why not this one? Plus, why only have one working drawer?"

"Maybe…" I started.

"Just help me and stop trying to come up with useless explanations," she snapped.

"If it hurries this up, fine." I knelt down beside her. We each grabbed hold of the handle and yanked with every bit of strength our feminine bodies possessed.

The drawer popped open with a loud scrape and groan. I fell on top of her and she burst our laughing. I rubbed my elbow where it had scarped across the carpet, scowling the whole time.

"Quiet." I sat up and looked inside; it was empty.

"Looks awesome; lot of room for useless junk," I said. I got to my feet. "Any other empty things you need help opening?"

I was in a mood now. We had so much to do, and wasting time with useless drawers wasn't one of them.

"It's not empty," she said. She held up a yellowed piece of paper. She began to silently read. Curiosity got the best of me. I sat down beside her and read it over her shoulder. It was almost completely full.

"Two different handwritings," I said as I read.

"Two vastly different people as well," she laughed. "One in love with some phantom person and one who clearly had or has some relationship issues."

14

"Neither are anywhere close to what love is," I said, getting back to my feet.

"We could correct it." She had a big smile on her face, like an excited child.

"Why?"

"Why not?" she asked, shrugging. I groaned; she had a point. I held out a hand and helped her up. She pushed the pile of clothes off the desk chair, ignoring my cringe as she did. She pulled the chair up to the desk and sat down. I sat on her lap.

"So…" I started to say, not sure exactly what we were doing.

She picked up a pen and began to write.

I love (maybe) how sarcastic you can get. Always trying to sound like things annoy you. You don't want me to know how little or how much you care about different things. I love (maybe) how you hide behind that mask. You wouldn't be you without it."

The paper was full. I pulled another sheet from the corner of the desk and wrote.

I love (maybe) how exasperating you are. You find excitement and frustration in the weirdest and smallest things. You love the rain and freak out because of an ant. I love (maybe) how I have to rescue you all the time.

I love (maybe) how you scowl when you rescue me, a scowl with a slight upward turn of the lips; like you are trying to not laugh. I love (maybe) how I sometimes do stupid shit just so you can rescue me.

I love (maybe) how that made me laugh. Maybe next time, I won't save you.

"Yes, you will." She laughed, capturing my lips in a kiss. I deepened the kiss and dropped the pen. She pulled away, held up a finger and pushed the pages into the drawer.

I grinned as she turned back to me. Decorating could wait.

****

"Don't wander too far away," my partner said.

"I won't." I sighed. Why did he think I would just walk off? I knew the risks; I knew losing sight of your partner could end only in death here.

We were in a rundown house, one of the last few to fall during the siege. The siege that had upended the world we once knew. Life went from going to work and taking care of families to hiding and allying with the toughest groups you could find in order to survive. The house wasn't burnt out like the rest, just trashed.

We were looking for anything that was salvageable: food, weapons, or even a book to take our minds off the mess around us.

So far we had found nothing but random crumpled pieces of paper, broken glass, and splinters of wood. This was looking like a useless excursion again.

I made my way down a dim hallway, to the last door on the right. The door was hanging off its hinge, as if someone had shouldered their way inside. I entered the room. It was just as much of a mess as the rest of the house. In a corner by the window sat the skeleton of what once had to be a bed. I scanned the room taking in the faded flowery decorations that bordered the walls. The only other piece of furniture left in the room was a desk in the very middle. Its surface was full of dust and dirt. I walked across the room to the desk.

I pushed the scraps of debris and dust from the surface and onto the floor, all that was left of someone's lost life. I ran my hand over the surface; it was smooth, barely scratched. I pulled open the top drawer; it had broken pencils, long-dead pens and half-empty staple boxes. Nothing of value.

The bottom drawer held a few notebooks, a handful of loose leaf pages, some more aged than others and a tangled mess of paperclips. I flipped through the papers, looking for something interesting. Two sheets with four different sets of handwriting caught my eye.   I pulled them out and sat on the surface of the desk. One sheet was very yellowed and barely legible. The other sheet was newer, just beginning to yellow and decay.

I skimmed the first portion. I smiled and laughed. The over-the-top wording brought up some man dressed in a Shakespearean outfit, proffering up a rose to a maiden up in a balcony.

My smile faded as I moved onto the second portion. The handwriting was neater, but there was anger here. The pen marks were almost etched into the paper. This poor person had been in so much pain but did all they could to pretend they were okay.

My eyes moved onto the third portion. The banter between the two people put the grin back onto my face. They reminded me of my best friend and me. We used to nitpick at each other like that. We loved each other with our whole hearts, but some stupid little things made us want to kill each other occasionally.

I stared at the last line, wishing it went on and on. I needed more to escape into. I sighed and glanced around the room; was there a working pen around here?

I spotted a white and black object under a broken board. I got up and went to inspect the object. I lifted the board, it was a pen with a white body and black cap. It was probably dead, but I might as well give it a shot. I grabbed the pen and went back to the desk.

I sat cross-legged on top and pulled the cap from the pen. I tested it on the corner of the newer sheet. There was still some ink left. I thought for a moment before I began to add to the odd tale.

I wish I could love like that heart. I wish I could one day love like I lived in a cheesy romantic comedy. I wish that one day, I would hear fake promises like those.

I wish I could hate like you once did. I wish I knew what it was like to have love break you into pieces. I wish that one day, I could tell someone I don't love them. I wish I knew what it meant to not love what someone does, so much that I can never forget them.

I wish I could love with that carefree attitude. We could tease each other, knowing we didn't mean a damn word we said. I wish I could love with laughter in my heart, in my eyes, and on my lips. I wish I could one day understand that love.

I wish love meant something anymore. I wish love was a word we still understood. I wish I loved something more than survival. I wish I loved.

Brittney RZ.

I sighed and gathered up the almost-full sheets. I felt my chest tighten. I couldn't cry where my partner might walk in and see. He would just tell me off. Strength was all that mattered anymore. I wiped the wetness from my eyes and slid the pages back into their home. Maybe, one day, these words would mean something again.

I got off the desk and went to find the rest of the team.

****

The desk sits in that room, waiting. Waiting for someone to open the drawers and find the pages waiting in its depths. Pages that hold all the ways that love can be experienced in a lifetime. The world changes as do hearts and how they feel and how they love. All those faces shared apart of their hearts onto those pages, and the pages will preserve those pieces so that one day love can live again.

I Like A Good Fight

LILA WASN'T A morning person. Bright sunshine and chirping birds only made her groan and bury herself deeper under the blankets. She was cocooned away and on the verge of falling back to sleep when she heard her apartment door open and close.

"You can hide all you want. I know you're in there." The voice was female. The voice of someone she had known since she could talk. It was her best friend Jessica.

"I'm half awake, and you know how this is going to end for you," came Lila's muffled reply from her little hole in the covers.

"You wouldn't dare." A swish of wind and a slap of cold air smacked Lila in the face as the covers were pulled from the top of her head. She moaned and curled up tighter into a ball.

"Give them back," Lila whined.

"No, have this coffee instead." Lila heard the covers fall softly onto the ground, and the edge of the bed sank down a few inches. Jessica tapped Lila's arm with the handle of the mug.

Lila peeked out from between her hands. It was a plain black mug, and wisps of steam floated up into the air. She could smell the heavenly scent of the dark Colombian blend.

Lila slid a hand out and grasped the mug. Sitting up on her elbow she took a sip. She felt the warm, bitter liquid sting her tongue and throat as it slid into her veins. Mornings weren't meant to be dealt with without this magical drink.

"Can we talk now, or do I need to give you a minute of privacy with that cup?" Jessica asked, grinning.

Lila pushed herself up to a real sitting position. Two hands grasping the mug, she rested her arms on the top of her knees.

"You may speak, but use small words and a calming tone" Lila said. "Caffeine hasn't fully kicked in yet." She kept the mug close to herself, the smell continuously tickling her nose and keeping her eyes open.

"It has been a week," Jessica stated.

"Oh, no—there isn't enough coffee or patience on the planet for that topic." Lila held up a hand. Jessica grabbed it and put it back at her side.

"You can't ignore it," she snapped.

"Yes, I can. I have been doing a damn good job of it, to be honest. *You* are the one who can't ignore it. *You* keep obsessing over it. I'm just fine over here in my ignorant little bubble." Lila sipped her coffee and tightened her grip on the mug to keep herself from tossing it at her best friend.

"It doesn't go away," Jessica said. "This is for real. This is your one shot."

Lila just gave her a shrug. If she was anyone else Lila would have thrown them out the door. No one told her what to do or when to do something. She didn't appreciate those always self-serving nuggets of advice. People said them to look good but never to actually help in the long run.

Jessica was her best friend, though. Since they learned to speak, they had been attached at the hip. They played the same sports, cried at the same movies, and got the same songs stuck in their heads. Lila swore they were clones; science just wasn't ready to present them to the world yet. Jessica was the only one allowed to bring up a topic as nauseating and frustrating as this one and not get a cup of hot coffee to the face.

"I decide when it's my one shot, not some damn app," Lila finally said.

"You know that isn't how it works anymore." Jessica reached out and grabbed her best friend's hand. "Please don't lose this."

Lila was done with her coffee. She threw her legs over the edge of the bed and walked out of the room, leaving a very frustrated Jessica behind her. She rinsed her cup and wiped a splash of water off the countertop.

"Dammit, Lila." Jessica was still in the bedroom.

"Not my name," Lila called back. "Today I'm just Lila." She went to the other side of the sink and began tidying the pile of papers that were slowly taking over the surface.

Jessica was silent for a moment. In about thirty seconds she would be in the kitchen. Lila put two piles together. She was about to begin ripping up the junk mail when she heard the footsteps.

"Right on time," Lila whispered to herself.

"You are a stubborn bitch sometimes, you know that?" Jessica wasn't shouting, but she was on the precipice.

"I do know that. You and many others tell me quite frequently." Lila went to the trash can and threw the junk mail confetti away.

"Do you want to be alone forever—is that it?" Jessica asked. "Come home to silence and emptiness? Have no one to talk to about anything? No one to break down around or cry with?"

"You know none of that is true, but I want to have that choice. I want to decide if and when I fall. I don't want you or some damn phone to tell me who I'm supposed to be with." She turned to her friend.

"Honey," Jessica's voice softened as she opened her arms and wrapped Lila in a warm hug. "You still get a choice; this just makes the process easier. Please, just give him one date. That's all," Jessica pulled away. "I just want to see you happy."

"Me too." Lila pulled herself out of her friend's grasp and walked into the hallway. "You're going to be late for work." She held the door open.

"Fine; I'll be back tomorrow," Jessica said as she walked to the door.

"And every day after that until I give in, I know. Going to be nice getting my coffee made for me every morning for eternity." She smiled.

Jessica laughed and walked out into the hallway. Lila closed the door softly behind her.

Lila went into her bedroom and began trying to find two socks that could potentially pass as matching. She had finally found a likely pair when her phone rang.

She picked it up from the bed and sighed as she answered it.

"Hello?"

"Hiya." It was him. He was as persistent as Jessica. Sometimes, she thought the program had screwed up and mispaired her. Jessica was meant for this man.

"What do you want?" she asked. It was still quite early in the morning, and she was still in bitch mode.

"One date." It was the same response every time he called. He called about this time every morning. She never told Jessica, knowing that would only fuel her fire. Her days were getting annoyingly predictable.

"Why?" she asked.

"Because you are my one." He sounded exasperated, probably because she made him state it every time he called. She let out a groan. God, did she despise that damn term.

The One was an app that had come out when she was still in high school. After years of research and experiments, scientists had finally figured out a way to determine your soulmate for you. Cancer still killed millions, and terrorists with bombs were still wreaking havoc across the globe, all because science was too busy helping you find that one "special" person. The world was going to hell, but hey, at least you wouldn't be alone when the fire and brimstone started falling from the sky. She was always amazed at the "problems" that the world chose to solve.

Her girlfriends had lost their damn minds when the news had come out. The slogan for the company who created the app had been "It's in your blood." She always hated that concept. She knew the saying, whenever someone was good at something or has a talent people would say, "It is in your blood." As if your blood holds a important piece of who you are as a person. One sample and they can deconstruct what makes you, you and find you your soulmate. She doubted the legitimacy of the process. But her friends did not share here fears or concerns. They were just so excited not to have to do the legwork anymore.

You got a notification announcing that your soulmate had been found. A picture and statistics were uploaded to your phone. The app celebrated a 90% success rate at pairing you up with the person you would marry. Jessica had never given up hope, while Lila had continued to pretend the whole thing didn't exist.

They had all done it together, and then they had waited and waited and waited. It had been years, and she was the first one to be given her true love out of the original group of friends.

Now she had been chosen, and her supposed true love was on the other end of the phone. Her friends and half the world would kill to be her right now. One less thing about life to struggle with and fight for.

"My name is Lila, not 'the one,'" she finally said.

"Fine, Lila, meet me for a drink. Give me one drink, and if I'm still getting on your nerves, we'll put this thing aside for a while," he suggested.

Lila knew he would never truly give up. Though with one drink, she could chase him to the hills, through a ravine, and into the abyss, never to be heard from again, at least by her. Fine. If he wanted to play, she would play, and she would make him wish he had never downloaded that damn thing.

"Fine, meet me at eight at Sam's. You get one drink, and then I'm gone. Forever." She made that last word hang in the air before she said, "Got it, Cliff?"

"Got it, Lila." He hung up.

Lila threw her phone onto the bed. It bounced up and got lost in the mess of pillows. She knew she should text Jessica and tell her what was going on, but she knew Jessica would make her promise to behave and give him a chance. Lila didn't want the lecture, and besides, she enjoyed the morning coffee service a little too much.

Lila arrived twenty minutes late. She hoped he would have left, making her job stupidly simple. But that would have been too easy. He was at the bar, hands steepled, occasionally glancing around.

She stood in the crowd, watching him for a moment. He was a handsome man with dark brown hair shaved close to his head. His jaw was covered in rugged scruff that made her smile, her one weakness in men. He wore faded blue jeans and a blue and green button-up shirt.

She made her way over and took the seat beside him. She was in jeans and a T-shirt, the same one she had worn all day. Her hair was combed back, the strands tucked behind her ears. She wore no makeup and no jewelry.

"Cliff?" she asked.

"Lila." He gave her a big smile. "Nice to finally meet you." He held out a hand to her.

Lila shook it. She was going to make him dislike her, but she wasn't going to be a real bitch about it. There was a certain line that she wasn't going to cross, no matter how much she despised this. He was just going to find out soon that they would never be able to work together. They had too different of personalities and would never be able to get along for a lifetime. That was what she wanted to make absolutely clear to this man.

"What drink would you like? And a real drink, not a shot. That won't count," he said.

Lila let a grin slip through. He wasn't dumb. "Fine, how about a simple vodka and cranberry?"

"Good choice." He singled to the bartender. He ordered her drink as well as a beer for himself. The drinks arrived a minute later. She sipped hers; it was mostly cranberry juice with just the barest hint of vodka.

"So what should we talk about? Favorite color? Movies? Job? Worst relationship?" he suggested.

"No, those are lame and boring. I don't care about your answers, and I know you don't care about mine." Lila was good with brutal honesty.

"Well, I'll have to learn the color thing sometime 'cause it will only end in a fight one of these years," he said, still grinning. "I'll get the answer wrong when we go out with friends, and you'll be pissed, and I'll end up sleeping on the couch because I don't know you at all. I hate the couch; it's not comfortable."

"Purple," she said, despite herself.

"Okay, I'll remember that." He took a sip. She copied him. "So what should we talk about, then?"

"Why did you download the damn thing?" she asked. If he got all gooey and cheesy on her, she could crush him with sarcasm and the cold shoulder. If he got all philosophical, she could get all rational on him.

24

His answer would determine the method she would use to destroy him.

"Because it's always intrigued my friends," he said. "I just went along with it at first." He began to peel his beer label.

Lila didn't respond. His answer hit too close to home. This wasn't an answer she knew how to react to. How was she supposed to counter that? Anything she said or did would be an insult to herself and her way of thinking. She could pretend to think that was ridiculous, but she wasn't going to tear herself down just to get rid of this guy. That was crossing the line.

"Why did you keep it after they all did it and not delete it right away?" she finally asked as a response; maybe he would help her out with an answer this time. She raised her glass to take a sip but stopped. It was a small glass, and she didn't have more than maybe a couple of mouthfuls left. She'd wait for his answer and then determine if she was going to gulp down most of the glass or pursue this thing little bit longer.

"Good question." He stared at the mirror behind the bar for a moment. "Curiosity, I guess? A small voice in my head that kept whispering, 'Just wait and see.' Then you popped up, and I thought, why the hell not? Let's see where this goes." He looked over at her. "Why did you keep it?"

"Because..." she stopped and took a small sip of her drink. She had just maybe one more mouthful left. "Because I'm lazy," she finally said. "Just never got around to deleting it."

"So you think this is bullshit, then?" he asked.

"Yep." She rattled her ice. "True love is meant to be hard. You fight for it from the very beginning. You fight through every wrong choice and decision until you find the right one, someone who makes all those dumb moves seem like nothing. You fight to knock out the kinks and find a way to live together. Then you fight to keep the damn thing alive for the rest of your lives. An app can't make true love possible." She threw back the last bit of her drink, hoping to erase the ache of confusion in her head. What was she doing talking like this with a stranger? "It's too easy." She stood up with quite a clear head. Clearly, there had been little to no alcohol in that drink.

"Good," Cliff said, "Because there is nothing I like better than a good fight." He winked at her and held out a hand.

Lila shook his hand, holding on for a moment before letting go.

25

Brittney RZ.

"Good night." She walked towards the entrance. Just as she got to the door, she looked back; he was watching her. He winked and waved good-bye.

She felt her hand rise, and she nodded as she waved back. She exited the bar and got into her car. She put the car into reverse as she sighed in defeat. As she pulled out of the space and headed to her apartment, she whispered, "Dammit."

ROGUE

MY PAPER WAS full of scratch marks. There were maybe two words that made it through my path of destruction, and that was only because they were names. I was getting beyond frustrated at this point. This was a pointless task; I was just wasting ink and paper.

Why was this so damn hard? I should be able to just write; the words should flow from my pen, and an hour later, I should have this beautiful story that would make people laugh and cry. But that was a nearly impossible task when the damn characters wouldn't stay in their places.

"NO!" The word appeared in the bottom right hand corner, the last white space that was left on this accursed page.

I should have just torn the sheet out, thrown it away, and left this whole ordeal behind me. I shouldn't have played this game with this idiot, but I found myself turning the page.

"Yes," I wrote, pen leaving an indent in the pages. "Now go to the background and stay there." In my head, I was swearing, words I'd never include in my prose.

"NO." The word appeared on the next line, big and bold.

"Dammit," I snapped. I scratched out the three lines. This page was just going to be a repeat of the last one. Why was I playing this game?

"Having fun yet?" the man asked. I didn't have to write out his description; I knew exactly how he looked. He was standing with his arms crossed, a small selfish smile spreading across his face.

"GO!!!!!" I wrote, all capitals and full of exclamation points.

"You can write a thousand of those; I'm not going to listen," he replied. He would be shrugging at me, his damn grin asking me why I

27

wouldn't give up on this fruitless argument.

"Why?" I finally wrote. I didn't want to have this conversation with him. I wanted him to do what I said, to float along in the back half of the story. He was just supposed to be a small little voice that came and went, nothing more. He didn't want that, obviously, and my threatening and pushing was getting me nothing but wasted paper.

"Because," he replied.

"Not good enough," I wrote back. "If you want a life, you'll explain, or I'll make you disappear." He might believe he was in control, but I still held the pen. I still held the paper, and I could crumble his world up and destroy him in one movement.

"Will that really solve the problem?" he asked.

I went to write back a snappy remark about me being the writer, which meant I could and would do anything, but I stopped myself. Arguing was nothing. I just had to prove my point.

I flipped the notebook over and began a whole new story. This one was set in the Middle Ages. A poor peasant woman came home from another day of monotonous work, which was done just to ensure the next day showed up. As always, she looked up at the castle on the hill, the place where the one person she loved most sat. She whispered a quick prayer before going inside and leaving that memory where it belonged.

A knock sounded at the door. Confused, she went to answer the door; she never got visitors, and no one was usually out at this hour. She opened the door to find a handsome man with a wide grin and bushy eyebrows.

"Hi." He waved, and I threw my pen across the room.

What the hell? Where did he come from? She was a lonely widow; no one was her friend. No one knew she existed, not even the son that resided in the castle. This was her story; it was about coming to terms with her decision and ultimately leaving the boy to a better life.

There was no Prince Charming. There was no casual, quirky friend to help her. She was alone; that was the whole point. So where the hell had this guy come from?

My pulse was quickening, and my muscles were getting tense. Frustration was boiling up inside my chest. I was the writer, dammit.

I got up, retrieved my pen, returned to my desk, found a new page near the back of the notebook, and began again.

This time, I set the story in the fifties. A young woman was packing up her suitcase, shirts neatly folded on top of slightly-faded jeans. She rolled up a couple pairs of socks and tucked them into the sides of the suitcase. She placed her toiletries bag right on top and shut the case.

She turned to the door and found her father in the doorway, a smile on his face. "He won't watch you leave. He is waiting in the living room." He moved out of the way and let her go into the living room. Her mind raced as she tried to determine who exactly this man was.

On the couch sat *him*, wearing a crisp white shirt, pressed slacks, and shiny shoes. The whole outfit was pulled together by the smartass smile on his face.

"Miss me?" he asked.

"NO!" I was on my feet, hands flat on the desk. I felt like I was spinning around and around. My heart was racing, my mouth was dry, and all I wanted to do was put my fist through the wall.

Why would he not go away? He didn't belong. He was not worthy of a story; why didn't he see that?

I should have left the room and poured myself a glass of wine. I should have taken a very long walk around the neighborhood. I should have eaten a whole bag of cookies while watching some mindless television show. I should have done a lot of things.

What I did was pick up a new pen, find a fresh new notebook, and sit in the very center of the room. I crossed my legs, clicked the pen, and wrote so furiously that I would never be able to read the chicken scratch lines later.

The year was 2031, and the world looked nothing like we know it today. Technology had taken over, and robots and computers did everything from grocery shopping to planning anniversaries. We just had to show up, have fun, and not think.

A young child sat on a fountain, watching the water change colors: red, blue, purple, and red again. He was waiting for his brother; they were supposed to walk home together. Their mother was a worrier, though in this day and age, that word was basically obsolete. Some people didn't evolve as fast, though.

He reached out to touch the synthetic water but quickly pulled his hand back. One moment he was staring at the clear surface the next it was marred by a pair of sleek sliver shoes. He looked up and laughed at the man, who was dressed in a shirt and pair of pants like someone from his history book would wear.

"Oh, come on," I groaned, falling back into the hard ground. This was just ridiculous now. He wasn't even trying to fit in anymore.

I stared at the spinning ceiling fan; the blades whirled around and around, distorting the colors and objects around them. I stared, mesmerized, not thinking. I wasn't going to let a single damn thought intrude.

Five minutes later, a stray thought crept its way into my head. A man sat at a bar, laughing at a joke that the bartender told him. She shook her head, exasperated at the person before her. He was trying too hard, but it was cute. The man wiped his mouth and looked to the right.

I shot up and screamed. I screamed as loud as I could. I screamed until my chest hurt, my throat was raw, and I had no breath left. I took a deep breath and screamed again. I was glad I lived in an isolated area, or the police would surely be knocking down my door by now.

"Just leave me alone," I pleaded. But I knew that was not going to happen until I gave in. He would continue to pop up over and over again until I either did what he wanted or completely lost my mind. Since I wanted to hang onto the little bit of sanity I still possessed as long as possible, I pulled my notebook back onto my lap and began to write yet again.

I wrote for an hour and a half. I tried to write his story in a variety of different ways. I made him the misunderstood hero; the angry, revenging villain; and the left-out sidekick, but I couldn't make anything work. I would get through the first few scenes and then falter. My words would start feeling forced and sound clunky. I'd scratch out the lines and try to restart from a new place but nothing was working.

"See? I can't do it. I told you," I wrote after my hand and brain started to cramp.

"I see," he replied. "Today does appear to be a wash. Well, there is always tomorrow. See you then!" I could just see him waving and whistling as he left.

"Bastard," I moaned. I got up and left my notebook and pen on the ground. I headed to my bed and collapsed without changing into pajamas. I closed my eyes. Hopefully, my dreams would give me either his story or a fabulously creative way to write out his demise. Either way would work for me, though I highly preferred the second.

Goodbye

THE KNOCK ON the door was loud and urgent. I got up from the couch, leaving the television on, a laugh track following me to the door. The person on the other side barely gave me ten seconds before they were hammering away at the door again.

"I'm right here," I muttered, trying not to let my exasperation seep out too much. Maybe the person was in trouble. Did I really want to be the bitch who yelled at a distraught stranger?

I was swinging the door open just as the knuckles came toward the wood once again. My best friend Macky's hand fell through the air and back down to her side. Macky stood there, silent, as she took in the last moment and comprehended that I had opened the door.

"Mac?" I asked, irritation swallowed by apprehension and confusion. She was standing, tear streaks staining her cheeks. "Hon, what happened?" I pulled her over the threshold, throwing glances to each side of the house. No one appeared to be around. I closed the door and threw the lock in place.

Macky was pulling her hands over her face. Her mouth was moving but no words came out.

"Come and sit down." I led her to the couch and carefully had her take a seat. She sat there, twisting her hands in her lap, not speaking.

I turned off the television, throwing us into silence. I knelt before my friend and grasped her hands in my own. Macky was normally a calm woman. She had the life many envied: the house, husband and career. Everything came easily to her, and she was always smiling and laughing. The woman that sat before me was not the woman I had known since the first day of ninth grade.

"I didn't mean to. I just didn't know what to do, so I put them away. I thought it was safe. Out of sight, out of mind. But it didn't stop them. There were just two, now I have four. I'm out of room. He's going to find them soon, and then what? What do I do?" She never looked away from me during her whole gibberish-filled rant.

I rubbed a hand over her wrist as I tried to decipher what she had just told me. They were all English words, but together, they made little to no sense to me. What was hidden away? How were there more? Were these things alive?

"Okay, you're going to have to start again for me. I got the part about hiding something, but who? What?" I asked.

"I can't. You won't understand. I shouldn't have come." She made to stand up, but I held tightly to her arms and kept her in place. She didn't try to escape again, just sat and stared.

"I can understand. You just need to give me something to work with here. What are we talking about?" I tried to make my tone harder, hoping to guilt her into explaining better. She was scared and frantic, not in her right mind. I had no idea how she had gotten to this point, but I wasn't letting her run off like this.

"I can show you better than I can tell you," she said, her voice full of tears.

"Okay." I stood up pulling her to her feet with me. She took it and stood up. I gathered her to my side and walked towards the door. I untangled us for a minute as I put my shoes on and found my keys under a pile of junk mail. Macky watched me the whole time, biting her nails and running her hands up and down her arms like she was cold.

"Let's go," I said softly and led her out through the door. I closed and locked it behind me.

"I'll drive." I took the keys from her palm and sat her down in the passenger seat. She didn't fight me; she sat and waited. I ran around the front of the car and into the driver's seat and started the engine. We had to get to her place fast, before she completely broke down, but I was nervous of what we were going to find there.

Twenty minutes later, we pulled into her driveway. I turned off the engine and waited patiently for Macky to make a move. I didn't know exactly where these four things were that were causing this breakdown. Were they in the garage, the attic, buried in the backyard?

Macky didn't move; she just sat staring at the house in front of her with wide, frightened eyes. I watched as her breathing got more shallow and staggered. Tears were free-falling down her cheeks, and a whimper escaped her lips. She just watched the house. Steeling herself to enter? Waiting for some signal from whatever was inside? Or had she snapped, fallen into some coma-like state?

I quickly reached over and grabbed her hand, hoping to ground her in some way. She grabbed on like I was a rope in a tossing sea. Her fingernails dug into the back of my hand.

I gave her another moment before I finally asked, "We going inside?" She nodded, eyes never leaving the face of the house. "Okay." I pried my hand loose and walked around to her side of the car. I opened the door. I don't know if it was the light breeze or the sound of the door clicking open, but she snapped out of her stunned state and almost jumped out of the car.

"Come on." She took my hand and began to pull me towards the house. I barely was able to slam the door closed. My throat was getting tight with apprehension. One minute Macky was on the verge of a panic attack, and the next, she was pulling me toward the house with all her strength, her face set and determined.

"We can get rid of them together." Her hand was on the door but didn't turn the knob. "Please, don't judge me too harshly when you see. Please." For a moment, her face fell back into the panicked, sad woman from earlier.

"Never." I clasped her hand with both of mine. She nodded and opened the door. As we entered, I sincerely hoped I wouldn't be eating my words in a few moments.

She pulled me up the steps to her and Jacob's bedroom. As we crossed through the doorway, I noticed how quiet the house was. It was almost seven; where was her husband? I didn't get time to think too hard before she rushed to the door farthest from the entryway.

She stopped and turned to me. "They're in here. He doesn't go in here ever. We have our own closets, and they are very quiet. They are scary-looking, but they listen really well." She gave me a small, sad smile. "I wish I could keep them."

I felt my mouth go dry. What was behind the door? Why did she go from sheer panic to sorrow, as if she was about to show me some wild animals she was being forced to return to the wild?

I pulled my hand back and had one foot poised behind me, ready to spin around and run. She was officially scaring me now. What did she have behind that door? What had she done? My chest was tightening, and my heartbeat was deafening me. I braced myself to run and scream when she turned and opened the door.

The scream came out as a squeak of surprise. Standing with heads bowed were some of the ugliest creatures I had ever seen. There were four, as she had stated before. The tallest one was green-skinned with a head that held two clumps of black hair. His hands were snarled, and a few stray strands of hair were sticking out of his fingernails. Beside him was one that was no more than a foot tall. He stood and stared up at me with wide, white eyes. His body was red and round like a ball with a few black spots peppering his back. He didn't look scary—more like an expectant puppy that was happy to see his master and ready to play.

Next to him stood one with bright blue skin and grey horns. His head bent almost to his knees, and he was shaking like he was standing on a fault line during an earthquake. His skin was almost translucent, enough to give me an nearly-clear view of his bones underneath. He never looked up; he just stayed in his bent form, whimpering quietly. I saw Macky twitch. Was she eager to bend down and comfort him?

Standing next to him was one that was black as midnight without any streetlights or stars. I could barely make out his body shape in the shadows. His eyes were bright, large silver orbs that beamed anger and suspicion at me.

"What are they?" I whispered, afraid, I'd get too loud and scare them. It was the appropriate question to ask. I had to keep up the act. Macky didn't seem to notice anything odd about my reaction, which was good. I had a role to play.

I didn't move, not sure how these ones would react to a new person. Were they just scared? Or were they more prone to attacking? I could see several long and harsh-looking claws. I would have no hope if they decided to take me out.

"I don't know." Macky pushed the door all the way open and casually walked over and sat on the edge of her bed. "Come on out, guys," she told them.

The round one jumped up and ducked down and rolled out into the room. Despite my fright, I laughed at him. I took a seat beside my friend as the creatures came out one by one. The tall one came out only a few feet before plopping down and staring out the window. The black-as-night one slunk out and came to sit at Macky's feet, keeping weary eyes on me the whole time. The blue one shuffled out and ran to Macky, winding his long, fragile-looking arms around her legs. She reached out and patted his head gently.

"He showed up first." She pointed at the tall one. "I had a mental breakdown and was screaming at the sky and throwing everything in utter frustration. I just couldn't take any of it anymore; the uncertainty and the confusion. Everything was swirling around me like a tornado and I had no control anymore. I broke. The next thing I know, he is in the closet, staring at me." Her voice was calm. She was no longer the sniveling, frightened mess that had showed up on my doorstep. The woman who was confused and scared felt comfortable among her new pets.

"He was last." She pointed at the black one. "Came through yesterday. He is sweet, but he is very protective of me. When he heard a dog bark, he growled that first day." She looked over at me, biting her lip. "I don't know what to do about them."

"Do they talk?" I asked her, watching the blue one shake and the red one squeal and roll around like a toddler.

"No, at least, they have never to me," she told me. "I mean, what do I do with them? Is there somewhere for them to go? Where are they even from? I mean, they showed up in my closet, and I just kind of adopted them. Am I losing my mind? I don't have any idea what to do." Her eyes were clouding over with tears again.

"I..." I had no words. A part of me was itching to tell her to light a match and let the whole place go up in flames and then bring in a priest to banish anything that the fire didn't take care of. I knew that treating them like pets was only going to let this all get out of control. We should not be sitting here watching these things like we had opened the door to find tiger cubs and wolves waiting for a friend.

It was easy to have that reaction at first. After the initial shock of seeing the creepy little guys, an attachment formed. They were sweet, just wanted to be your friend. But I knew that was the last thing they were. They were not and could not become pets.

I felt myself slipping, panic settling in my chest. One became two which became three, which just continued to grow until they were in control. They had to go, now before more came. Macky could not keep them, I would not let this happen to my best friend.

"I can't keep them. Jake will freak out, probably try to kill them." The black one growled and wound one claw around her pant legs. "Shhh..." she cooed at him. "But I can't just shove them out the door. What would they do? Where would they go?" Her lips were trembling, and she was on the verge of breaking down again. "I don't know what to do. I know this is insane, but I like them. They're fun and they need me, right?"

"Mack," I sighed. She saw these things as fun, exotic animals, but they weren't. They were... I couldn't even find a proper term for them. I had seen this once before, seen how they built up, one letting another in until you had no room left for them. Soon, her life would be ruled by these guys, and she would have no say on what she said or did or even thought about. I loved my friend too much to watch her go through that struggle to keep them and maintain control.

"They have to go." I let the words fall out cold and low. The black one narrowed his eyes at me. "And I know how," I told her.

She gave me a pained look. "You do?"

"Yeah, I've done this once before." I felt the words fall, each one piercing my heart. I struggled to keep myself in check. She didn't ask me where or with who and for that I was grateful. It as a long story that I didn't think I could explain. There were just some things that you never told anyone, even someone you considered your sister.

"Come on," I told her. There was no use putting this off. Macky stood, taking the blue and black ones by the hands. The tall one stood and followed when it saw that we were leaving the room. The red one squeaked and tumbled after us.

I led the way to the sitting room and over to the fireplace. Macky followed, turning on two small table lamps. I heard her breath hitch in her chest when she saw me move the grate from in front of the fireplace.

"No," she whimpered. I didn't look over at her as I grabbed a few fire-starting logs from the bricks beside the wall. I arranged them in place and struck a match from a book I found on the mantle. The logs caught almost instantly, and within a minute, I had a large fire blazing.

I stood back and finally turned to her. Her shoulders were shaking, and she was trying to hold back her cries. She held the blue one tightly to her side, like a mother who is in a crowd and doesn't want to lose her child. She kept shaking her head and whispering, "No."

"It's the only way. If you tell them to, they will go," I told her.

"Why?" It came out broken.

"Because they will only grow and breed more. You can't handle it, trust me. End it all now before you have no control over them." I felt my hands clench into fists and a twinge of guilt course through my chest. The way she looked at me you would think I was asking her to put down a beloved pet; one who had been aggressive only once. But I knew what the potential these things held and they just could not remain in her life.

"Macky," I commanded her when she still hadn't moved or spoken. "We can't just stand here," I told her.

"No." She shook her head side to side, whipping her hair around. The black one growled at me, showing me his small razor teeth. He was acting tough, but he never left Macky's side.

"Do it, or I will," I told her, straightening my back and clenching my hands into fists. "It would be better for them if you let them go instead of me forcing them away."

"I can't," she pleaded.

"Fine." My hand shot out, and I grabbed the tallest one's arm and tugged him to the edge of the flames. He let out a surprised gasp but nothing more. He did not look at me, keeping his eyes on Macky only.

Macky lunged forward and grabbed his shoulder. I had the better grip. All I had to do was tug once, and he would be in the flames. "Last chance," I told her.

"Fine," she whimpered, and I released the creature.

She pulled him close and kissed one of his tuffs of scraggly black hair. "I'm sorry," she mumbled, holding him tight. The blue and black ones still clung to her sides. The red one sat with legs spread out in front of him, watching the proceedings and no longer looking excited.

"Mack," I demanded.

She swallowed hard, said, "Go on," and turned the tall one around. He nodded and walked into the flames. He didn't flinch and didn't scream as the fire washed over him and swallowed him whole.

"Next." I pointed. Mack didn't even try to stop the tears that were now constantly flowing down her cheeks. She knelt and patted her knee and the red one scurried over and jumped up, tongue hanging out of his mouth. Macky let out a choked laugh and patted his cheek gently.

"Goodbye, little guy," she told him. "Go on." He gave her hand a kitten lick and stood up on her knee. He bent his own knees and leapt into the flames, his arms flailing and a giggle leaving his lips as the flames claimed him, as well.

I didn't speak as she turned to the black one, who no longer looked angry, just sad. His eyes weren't shining and his teeth were hidden away. She cupped his cheek and he nodded not waiting for her to speak. He walked forward and was gone.

The blue one was shaking so hard that I was surprised he was still standing.

"Come here." Her voice was no longer wavering. There were still tears falling down her face, but she was calmer now. "I know it's scary, but you will be okay. I promise." She kissed his head. "Goodbye, my friend."

He looked up, and I caught a glimpse of his face. He had small, pinched eyes and a little button nose. His lips were thin, almost nonexistent. He let them spread into a small smile and held his arms out. Macky wrapped him in a tight hug. She didn't want to let go; I could see that, but finally, he pushed away, patted her cheek, and turned around to follow his friends into the fire.

She didn't stand when he disappeared; she just watched the flames dance for a moment. Finally, she used the backs of her hands to wipe away her tears and took a few deep breaths.

"Thank you," she said as she stood up and held her arms out for a hug.

I walked into her embrace. "You're welcome," I sighed into her shoulder.

She opened her mouth, probably to invite me to stay for pizza and a movie, but I cut her off. "I'm tired."

"You can take my car home. When Jake gets home from his

business trip tomorrow, we'll come pick it up. I don't think I want to go out for a bit, anyway," she told me, putting the fire grate back in place.

"Thanks."

My house was pitch black when I got back. I had rushed out, not having had time to leave any sort of light on and not knowing that it would be night before I got back. I pushed open the door and instantly hit the hall switch to light up the foyer. I pulled off my shoes and made my way to the living room, making sure every light was on as I went.

In my living room, I stood and stared at my own fireplace, and my hands fiddled with the matches in my pocket. I pulled one out, lit it, and held it in front of the logs for a moment. But my fingers could not let it go. I brought it to my lips and blew it out, the thin wisp of smoke curling up to the ceiling.

RESET

RESET. THE WORD caused my muscles to tense and my throat to dry out. I tried to speak, but the words got lost before leaving my mouth.

"We have done all that we can. This is the only option we have left." The doctor's voice was low and full of sympathy. I found myself wondering if it was genuine or just well-practiced.

"And if we don't do it? Then what?" I asked, trying with all I had to keep my voice steady. I was asking the question more out of desperation then actually needing an answer. I knew what his response was going to be, and it would not be one that would ease the ache in my chest.

"He will die." He said the words slowly and carefully, as if making sure that I picked up on every single syllable. I nodded, showing that I comprehended the answer. I couldn't speak. My body was in the room, but my brain was not focused. That one terrible word just kept repeating over and over like some sadistic chant.

"When can we do the procedure?" His mother's voice came to my ears hollow and echoing as if she shouted the words from down a tunnel. I turned and stared at his mother. She was clutching her husband's hand tightly, but her face was set and determined. "Can we do it today? Or is there some sort of prep and wait time?"

"What?" I spluttered out, confused and taken aback. "Are you serious? We don't even get time to think this through?"

"We do not need time, and you don't get anything," she said, never looking over at me.

Her words were like a whip across my chest. This was a pain I should be used to by now, but every biting remark still hurt. We were not

43

friends, barely two people who could stand each other for more than a few moments. It was always curt nods and harsh words whenever we were around each other. I was never and would never be good enough for her little boy. I wasn't pretty enough, wasn't successful enough, wasn't smart enough, and wasn't so many other things that she never would be able to express them all in one sitting. A small part of me wondered if she was choosing this option to help her son or to spite me.

"When can it be done, Doctor?" she asked when I didn't reply to her comment.

I watched as the doctor winced and began to shuffle the papers on his desk, eyes refusing to look at the three of us. "It can be done as early as tomorrow. But I think Miss Macintyre is right. You should think this through. There is a reason this option is allowed on a last resort, desperation basis only. It will save your son's life, that is true, but who will you be getting back?"

"My son has been deteriorating for too long," she threw back. "I've watched you pump him with chemicals. I've anxiously sat hours in a dim waiting room while you cut into him. My husband and I were always praying and hoping that this time would be the last time. He has been in a coma for a month. The cancer is stealing him away. What is there to even think about?"

Her husband squeezed her hand in solidarity throughout her whole speech. The doctor nodded. I was sure he had heard this monologue numerous times before.

"I understand. I know this is difficult, but—"

"No, it really isn't," his father cut across. "We have this option, and it will save his life. Pretty simple."

"You aren't saving him!" I was on my feet now. The doctor gave me a warning look, one that said, *Take a seat; you are not going to help the situation.* But I didn't care. They needed to hear me.

"If you do this reset, you are taking away three years of his life. They will go in and take away all those memories. Every cry, every angry outburst, and every declaration of love will be gone. Do you understand that? They'll reset him, like some damn computer. His body will heal and return to its state before this all started, but you are destroying a part of him. You are making that choice. Not him, not fate. You." I was glad that my voice remained strong. My face was dry, and

44

my hands were not shaking.

"There is no choice." His mother stood, walked around the chairs, and came to stand face to face with me. "He left us in charge of his medical decisions, not you. He dies in a week or two, or he lives. Do you really see a choice here? Yes, he loses memories and has to adapt, but he will live. And I will not lose my son if I can do a damn thing about it."

"But what about me? The reset will erase me! I am the love of his life, and you will be getting rid of that!" This time I couldn't hide my fear. "I will lose him."

"You will lose him either way," she said.

"Just walk away," her husband said. "Don't stay and try to force the relationship. Let him move on." He paused, then whispered, "As he should."

I ignored him. "I can't live knowing he's alive but can't remember me. Do you know how much it will hurt to look at him and just see another face in the crowd? I won't survive that," I told her. I reached out to grab her hand, she put it behind her back.

"My concern is not for you." She turned back to the doctor. "What do we need to sign?" The doctor nodded and stood up.

"I will return with the necessary papers." As he moved towards the door, he placed a hand on my shoulder and guided me out of the room. I tried to turn around, but he wouldn't allow me to escape his grasp.

"Don't," he commanded as he closed the door behind him. He steered me to a file cabinet and opened the top drawer. "She can't hear you. She only hears and see her little boy being able to live again. To her, nothing else matters. You must understand that?"

"Of course I do." I nodded. I knew none of this was her fault. It was her job to protect her child, and that was exactly what she was doing. She had to think about the full picture while I was only focusing on one small corner. But that did nothing to lessen my pain.

The doctor closed the drawer, and I turned to leave the office. I wasn't sure where I was going to go. Home to cry? To his bedside to say goodbye? Would that even matter by tomorrow? To wander the streets? I barely heard the doctor call, "Wait!"

I stopped and looked back at him. He waved me back to his side. "I know this is not easy for you. I know you are feeling lost, not sure how to live on. Those memories they are going to take from him, but you have to live with them, and they can be life destroyers." He placed a card in my hand.

"Just in case." He closed my fingers and patted my hand.

I wasn't sure what I was supposed to do. I didn't look at the card, fearful of what it would say. I just nodded and turned back towards the door. As I reached for the handle, I heard the door to his office close behind me.

I didn't go to his bedside. I didn't need one more ache to tear at my heart and chest. He couldn't hear me, anyway, and I did not want to add one more final, torturous memory to my collection.

It wasn't until I got home that I really looked at the card in my hand. It was all white with only a line of text.

Need to start over? We can help with that.

The only other thing on the card was a phone number. I reached for my phone, dialed, and waited anxiously as the phone at the other end rang.

It was an ordinary Saturday. The bus was packed with people going downtown for a visit to the museums, a meal out by the lake, or just a bit of window shopping.

The woman was out of breath as she joined the end of the line of people waiting to board. She had just put her foot on the bottom step when someone knocked into her shoulder.

"Oh, sorry." A man smiled at her, stepping back.

She smiled back and said, "No problem." She turned and walked up the steps.

The man watched as she boarded the bus and it rolled away from the curb. As he watched it leave, he blinked a few times. He shook his head and turned to head up the street. But no matter how hard he tried, he could not shake the weird feeling that he somehow knew that woman.

KEEP THEM

"ARE YOU FUCKING serious?" she screamed, jumping up from the kitchen table. He watched her without a word or movement. His face remained stoic and calm. He was not angry, was not upset. He looked almost as if he couldn't be bothered. She resisted the urge to slap some emotion onto his face.

"Calm down," he instructed her like a teacher. She slammed her chair into the table.

"Shut up," she fumed. "Don't tell me what to do." She wrapped her arms around her chest and began to pace. "How is it we always end up having this same argument over and over again?"

The last question was aimed more at herself than at him. Month after month she found herself fuming and screaming while he sat smug and calm. She would start an argument and somehow he always turned the topic around to make her think she was in the wrong. She would fumble around until she had nothing left in her and then deflate. He would hug her, accept her apology and they would end up back in their places all over again.

"You tell me." He remained calm, eyes watching her dig a path into the floor.

She found her lip curling as she passed by his chair. Who did he think he was talking to? A teenager?

"Stop making this seem like a problem that is all about me," she bit back at him. "You are at fault here."

"For what?" He sat back and raised an eyebrow at her.

"Everytime I leave this house, it becomes an interrogation. You don't trust me, and I can't handle the surveillance anymore." She stopped pacing. "The constant phone calls. The insistence that I text and check in multiple times throughout the night. The third degree for ever phone call and text message. The wondering who I'm chatting with online all the time. It is beyond ridiculous. Hell, my parents weren't as 'concerned,' about me as you are. I don't do it to you."

"I've never given you a reason to do it to me," he told her.

"And I've never given you one either. Ever!"

"I just…"

"Don't even start with that shit again. You are just a paranoid crazy who has to be in control. I'm so done." She threw up her hands.

"I'm just being protective."

"No, you are being possessive," she countered. "And I'm not a thing you own. I'm done.We're done." She turned to leave, but he jumped up and grabbed her arm.

"Wait," he told her. She tugged her arm back to her side.

"Why?" She took a step away from him.   "You want to end this? Give up everything we've created?" he asked her. She locked eyes with him and nodded.

"Fine." He turned and left the room. She stood beside the table and waited. A tingle of fear slid down her back. He could not be doing what she feared. He would not sink that low, no one could sink that far. If he walked back through that doorway, holding it, she knew there was no salvaging this relationship. There was a line and he was dancing on the very edge.

When he came back into view with the grey steel box, with two key holes set in the lid, in his hands she felt her eyes start to tear up. He could have come back with any sort of weapon and this is what he had chosen. The devil knew exactly what he was doing.

"Put it away," she told him. "Leave it alone. Please."

"No, you want to end this? Fine. We will start the divvying up of possessions right now, starting with these lovely dreams, hopes and fears." He gave her a crooked smile that seemed to darken his eyes.

She blinked rapidly trying to hold in her tears. It was noon on a sunny summer day but the room was suddenly dark and cold.

"No." She threw up her hands. He thought he was being clever. He knew that once he opened that lid she would be trapped. "I'm not doing this." She made to leave the room again, but he blocked her path.

"We have no choice."

"Yes, we do. We can leave them alone. If you ever cared about me, even a small bit, you will stop this."

"No, we can't. If you leave, they can't stay."

She bit her lip. He was right; the box was no longer theirs to share. Breaking up always included splitting up possessions: couch, televisions, books, and kitchen utensils. Those things she could keep or part with without an issue. It was what lay in that box that scared her; the dreams, hopes, aspirations, and fears gathered over the years.

She hadn't wanted to combine their boxes at the start of the relationship. She had been nervous about mingling such important parts of who they were together. She had fought hard for a long time, always coming up with one excuse or another. He had finally broken her down, asking if she was really dedicated to the relationship. Did he not mean anything to her? He would ask over and over again everytime she refused to combine the boxes.

She had caved finally, the tears and pleas too much to handle. She was dedicated and wanted the relationship to succeed. But there was a small part of her that screamed in protest when they had finally combined the boxes. There was still a part of her that did not want to share, that wanted to hold something for herself and herself only.

"Let me go," she whispered, still trying to edge around him.

"No, if you want to leave, you have to see what you are leaving behind." He smiled and pulled her back to the table. Reluctantly, she sat in the chair where this had all started. She felt trapped. The door was only a few feet away but if she ran now she would be leaving too much behind. He had a point. She needed to see what was in that box, to know if she could walk away. Did any of what was in those depths matter anymore?

"Key." He held out his palm. She didn't move. His hand remained completely still, waiting. He would not let her leave until he had what he wanted.

"Here." She reached into her pocket and slapped the small piece of metal into his hand.

"Thank you." He smiled as he fished out his own key. He placed them both into their slots, side by side, and twisted them at the same time. The lid clicked and popped open a half inch.

"Ready?" he asked, a sinister smirk on his lips.

"No," she answered, knowing it would do nothing to deter him from the game he was playing with her. If he thought she was going to be a sobbing pathetic mess, begging him to leave it alone, he was wrong. She knew what he wanted and it was the last thing he was going to get from her. She took a breath and steadied herself.

"Too bad." He opened the lid and instantly, the kitchen was gone. They were now standing on a manicured lawn in the backyard of a small house. A waist-high wooden fence wrapped the property. She glanced to her left to see him smiling and nodding to the corner of the yard. She had seen and was trying to ignore the swing set, but he wasn't going to allow that. She turned and walked to the far corner. There on the swing set was a small girl, laughing as her parents pushed her higher and higher.

"The daughter we always wanted. This home, safe and content. You walk away from me, she disappears." He held her tight onto her arm as the copy of him in the dream kissed the little girl's cheek as she swung pass him.

She didn't speak for a moment. Instead she watched as the little girl swung back and forth. The girl was about five, a wide smile on her face, hair in two long pigtails. She watched as the dream copies of herself and him grinned down at the little girl.

She prepared for a tear to slip down her cheek. She waited for her chest to tighten and ache, watching her dream play out in front of her eyes. A dream she she was now being shown that she could not have. But the feeling never came.

"Hurts doesn't it? Seeing what could have been?" he asked, hand still tight on her upper arm as if afraid she was going to try to run off.

"I'm okay," she nodded. And she wasn't faking. She wasn't breaking down, wasn't having a panic attack. "Next?" she asked. His selfish smirk slipped. She knew he expected tears and desperate pleas. She watched the child fly up into the air, knowing this scene was sweet but just not quiet right. There were many ways to see this and this one was just one of them.

"Alright," he let her go and rubbed his hands together. The scene around them began to fade. The green grass faded to grey and the child swung up into the air then disappeared into the clouds. The copies of her and him faded. The backyard disappeared and an office came into focus.

They stood in a corner beside the only door to the room.

She watched as a tall woman in a black pencil skirt and white blouse stood before a giant window looking down at what was most likely a city street. He didn't speak, just let her watch for a moment. She crossed her arms, waiting to see where this was going.

An intercom buzzed. "Mrs. Larkinson?" The woman turned, it was her, a bit older but definitely her. She walked over and answered. "Yes?"

"Your one o'clock meeting is here. I also have the reports you wanted."

"Thank you," she answered. "I will be out in a minute." Her professional copy sank into the chair at her desk and typed for a moment.

He walked over and sat on the edge of the desk, hand clasped between his knees. "This is nice. Interesting view. Big office." She walked to the window and watched the people below scurry back and forth.

"What is your point?" She liked the feeling she got standing here watching the world below. It felt good seeing herself being in control, making the world wait on her for a change.

"How do you think you got here?" he chuckled with his next words. "Hard work? Years of struggle?" He shook his head. "No, no, no. I got you here. A bit of money passing between a few palms. A few well chosen words and you went from fetching coffee to drinking that coffee."

She knew she shouldn't but she could not hold in the laugh that was bubbling up in her chest. She laughed hard holding her side as she watched a bird fly up into the sky. So this was the game he was playing? Show her scenarios where he made something happen for her. He was going to manipulate and spin these scenes, try to make her think he had power over her life and her choices.

She turned to him, only chuckling now. He was glaring at her, smugness gone. She walked to him and stood face to face to him. "Good try. Fun game. But you lose."

"Excuse me?"

"You heard me. You think I believe for one minute that all this came from you? And if it did do you actually believe I would want it after all that?" she asked him.

"Without me you will stay the secretary."

"No, I won't. I will get this office, without you. I do not need you

51

to go anywhere. I will be in control. I will get here through my own hard work and talent. You will have nothing to do with it. Understand?"

She watched as his fists clenched and unclenched on his knees. "Got anything else?" she taunted. She knew she was walking a dangerous line. He could snap and attack her, but she also knew he was much more talk than action.

"Yes." He stood and grabbed her elbow.

The bright office disappeared, and into view came a small apartment. It was dark and the only light came from a computer screen in front of her. The copy of her here was wearing a large hoodie and ripped jeans. Her hair was in tangle, and she was lazily eating a bag of chips as she browsed through random websites. The crumbs coated her legs and the seat around her. She took a quick look around and saw how trashed the place was. There were empty food wrappers, dirty footprints and discarded clothes coating the floor.

"Wow, I see you are getting desperate." She shrugged. "This was a good try. This was the first fear I shared right? The first thing I took from my box and allowed to find in a new home in yours. Remember that night?"

"Clearly. You looked into my eyes, yours full of tears and confessed how scared you were that you could end up completely and utterly alone. You told me how happy you were to find someone and let this fear go. That you were happy to let me hold it for you."

"And now you are trying to use it as a weapon. This is low, even for you."

"Walk out that door and this is what is waiting for you." S h e opened her mouth to shout at him. She wanted to scream that he was insane. She wanted to berate him for playing this game with her. He was supposed to be the one person she trusted above all others. He was supposed to erase the fears and help her nurture her dreams and aspirations. Instead he did the exact opposite, using her fears against her and trying to manipulate her dreams until they were unattainable without him. She could scream and rant until she had no voice but she knew it would all fall on deaf ears.

Instead she shrugged, sighed and said, "Fuck you." She felt herself smile at his shock. She had feared this years ago, when she was lost and trying to live everyone else's lives. She was not that woman anymore, no matter what he may think.

She walked up to him, smiling wide. She snapped her fingers, and they were back in their kitchen. She blinked twice as the room came back into focus.

"Thanks for the tour." She stood up. "I'll go get some boxes so I can start packing."

"What about these?" he asked, hand slightly shaking as they gripped the steel box.

She walked over and slammed the lid shut, barely missing his fingers. "Keep them." She patted his shoulder and walked down the hall and out the door.

WHOLE AGAIN

MY ASSISTANT PEEKED his head around the door and gave me a sympathetic smile, "You have another one," he said.

"Another?" I looked up from the pages on my desk.

"Yeah, she's a frequent flyer." He told me, still just his head looking around the corner, probably waiting to see if I was going to get frustrated and start throwing the objects from my desk. "Emma something? You've dealt with her before, I think,"

"No, I haven't." I stood up and began to gather my things together. "But I know of her. She's gone through about eight of us and no one wants to deal with her anymore." I opened my drawer and slid the stack of pages inside.

"Oh." My assistant nodded in understanding. There was only one reason I got a call. When someone was on their last chance I was given their file. I went in and decided if they were given one more shot to take care of their hearts.

"Broken or dented?" I asked as I slipped on my tennis shoes.

"Apparently shattered." He saw that my fingers weren't itching towards a stapler or phone and decided it was safe to come into full view. He moved to the doorway and leaned against the jamb watching me get ready. "The paper says pieces are everywhere and barely anything is left intact. Is there anything you can actually do?" He asked as I shrugged on my jacket.

"I always hope there is but rarely do I get to see that hope live." He nodded and headed back around the corner to his office. I followed.

"Can't say I envy your job," he told me as he sat back down in his

55

chair. "Good luck."

"Thanks." I couldn't make myself sound anything but exasperated.

The journey was short. I knew the location. It was pretty much a permanent dot on our maps nowadays. I knocked on the door and waited patiently for Emma to answer. As I waited I looked around. Her porch was almost too clean. There was barely any dirt or dust on the wooden floor and the chairs looked brand new, no rust or scratches. I sighed. Too bad she couldn't take care of her heart as well she took care of her porch.

"Oh it's you," she said as she opened the door. No greeting or hello, no smile. I nodded. She opened the door wider and I stepped inside. "It's in the living room." I went down the hall and through the doorway. She didn't follow me.

The coffee table was upended, magazines and food wrappers littered the ground. Mixed in with the crumbs and torn pages were the pieces of her heart. I knelt down and began to gather the pieces into my palm. Some were so small only I would have been able to find them.To some they just look like slivers of glass or plastic, but I had been doing this for quiet awhile. I knew what I was looking for. I tapped the pad of my finger on a piece that was nothing but a speck. How were we going to piece this mess together again?

We were good. We could take a broken heart and mold the remaining piece together perfectly. No seams, no cracks and no tears. It would look exactly as it had the day the owner had been presented with it.

As I gathered the shards, slivers and specks I wondered what part of "Fragile, handle with extreme care," no one understood. What else could those words mean? Nowhere did it say, 'Please throw me around like a softball," or "No worries, jut shove me in a drawer, I'll be just fine." We warn them, we give them the option to have ownership of their hearts or to leave them in our care. And every damn time they choose to take their hearts out of storage, we get a repair call. One is fine, we all make mistakes. Twice is annoying but we understand and it's okay. Some people are just slow learners. But this situation is beyond ridiculous. You would think this woman liked feeling broken.

"A mess right?" I heard her muffled words from the doorway but didn't initially turn around. I finished gathering the last few pieces and tucked them inside a bag I had on my hip. After they were secured I stood up and faced the owner of the disaster.

I hadn't paid too much attention to her when I had first walked in, more concerned about the situation at hand. Now I got a good look at her and I can't say I was too surprised. She looked like she hadn't gotten out of bed in days. Her hair was a nest of tangles on the top of her head. It would take hours of brushing and even possibly require some cutting to fix the mess. Her cheeks were sunken deep black shadows, and stuck our strikingly against her pale as snow complexion. She looked exactly like you'd expect someone to look who had torn her heart to pieces and left them in a heap.

"Yes, a mess is a light way to put this," I told her.

"I haven't ever seen you before."she said, arms crossed on her chest. "I just recognized your uniform." Her voice was so hollow, it made me squirm.

"Well, I rarely make house calls. I'm senior level, I generally do paper work. I get called in for difficult cases." I didn't want to say hopeless out loud, but right now that was what this situation seemed like to me. I didn't tell her that rarely was I brought in for a case that could be solved and didn't end in confiscation.

"Ha," she laughed, shocking me. "Difficult. That doesn't even begin to cover me. Why don't you cut the crap and tell me exactly what you are here to do? Can you really fix that? Or am I just screwed?"

"Where is the rest?" I asked her, trying to dodge the moment when I had to tell her the inevitable.

"In the box." She walked in and picked up the wooden box that had made its way under the side table. She opened it to show me what was left. Sitting on the velvet was too chunks of her heart. From a quick glance I couldn't even start to tell what parts they were. This was going to take months if we even tried.

"See? It doesn't even resemble anything recognizable anymore." She sat down on her couch, her shoulders falling. "Why are you even bothering?" She asked quietly as I closed the box and tucked it under my arm.

"Because it is my job," I told her. It was a hundred percent the truth. I worked to repair what others couldn't.

"Of course and you can't look at something and say it is hopeless. Wouldn't look good for you guys would it? Can't say, 'Nope, not even going to bother with this one. Here are your pieces, have a nice day.' They wouldn't pay you would they?"

"I get paid no matter the outcome. We like to at least give a repair a try," I told her. She nodded.

"Some part of me appreciates that." She stood up and led me to the door. "When can I expect it to be done and returned?" She asked as she held the door open for me.

I bit my lip. "Well…" How was I going to say this? "The repair itself should take a month, if we can actually fix it."

"So I'll have it back in a month no matter what? Alright." I didn't walk out.

"No," I told her. "You won't be getting it back. If we can fix it we will place it in our storage unit where it will be safe. If we can't completely fix it we will still put it away in storage until we can find donor parts to try to make it functional again. Either way you won't be getting it back. You can repeal the decision but it is unlikely you'll win. We can't trust you."

"Wait." She slammed the door in my face. I didn't flinch. This wasn't the first time I had stood in this place about to have this shouted conversation. "Are you telling me that you are keeping my heart indefinitely? You can't do that! It's mine!"

"It was yours, and you are allowed to keep it as long as you take care of it. It is in the contract you signed when you checked it out. You knew what was expected of you and you ignored all of it. We have given you too many chances. Look at what you have done? We can't trust you anymore. It is ours now. We put a lot of time and energy in to preserving and taking care of these things and we are don't appreciate our clients destroying them." I tried to move to the door but she moved in front of it and stood still.

"I tried! How can you expect me to be able to just leave it alone all the time!?" she asked me.

The desperation was always the same. Always the same questions. How could we expect them to control themselves? The temptation was too strong. What were you supposed to do when you could see your pain and joy day in and day out? How could you resist poking and prodding at it? Trying to see what it could take.

Trying to see what did what to it. I always responded the say way. "Most of our clients manage it somehow."

"Well aren't they just fucking special. I can't be them. I'm not them. Sorry, I screwed up. I'm human...," I held up a hand.

"Going to stop you now." I held her gaze. "I've heard it all. Trust me you have no new excuses to shout out. So don't waste your breath or my time. You were given a chance. You knew the consequences. Now I'm going to leave and you are going to let me." She opened her mouth to argue but I cut her off again. "I seriously don't have time for this. Just let me leave. Trust me it will be better with us in charge of your heart. You'll see."

She stared at me hard for a second. I never blinked. She dropped her head and stepped aside. I opened the door and just as I left I heard her whisper. "You're probably right." I closed the door and jogged down the steps to my car.

I arrived back at the office just as my assistant was leaving. "How did it go?" He asked as he grabbed his keys.

"Confiscated. Repair will be long and difficult but I think I can do it." I told him as I headed back to my office.

"Of course you can." He gave me a knowing smirk.

I didn't say anything back. I walked into my office and went to the side closet. I unlocked it and turned on the light inside. Rows upon rows of boxes stood staring down at me. Each one was a heart confiscated by me. I pulled out a top drawer and emptied the pieces from the bag inside. All of them but one.

I picked up a sliver and held it in the light. It was the brightest one, it almost glowed. I could feel the warmth emanating from it.

"Perfect," I whispered. I closed the door, locked it and went to my bottom drawer. I pulled up the fake bottom and put the code into the safe underneath. The lid popped and I opened it. Inside sat a patchwork heart, my patchwork heart. Two dark shadows stood out. I slid the sliver into place at the very top. I sat back on my knees and admired my work. There was just one small hole left. Just one more piece and I would be whole again.

THE END

LEAVE HIM.
OR
Have a fight with no end.

The choice sat before her on the crisp white paper, the large black letters that should have been nothing more than lines. They shouldn't have had the power to destroy her entire life.

She chews her bottom lip as she reads over her options. She has a choice to make. If she doesn't choose, the words will haunt her, digging into her brain and lying there waiting for just the right moment to explode. Soon, they will be all she see or thinks about. Her world will be completely filled by these two options.

Once she opens her mouth and speaks the words out loud, she knows there is no turning back. As soon as the last syllable leaves her lips, the result will come to life before her. Paragraph after paragraph will fill the page, detailing exactly how her life will deteriorate.

She could walk away from him and the love they had managed to cultivate into a beautiful bloom. It could be a simple parting. They could stay friends, and her heart would ache but not break. She laughs at herself; that was dumb. She knew better. This damn book didn't give her the easy path. It took a shot to the gut that crumpled her into a ball and left her withering.

The other choice had much more daunting prospects. *A fight that would never end.* They would be together, but they would be angry all the time. Their love would struggle to breathe for months before it finally curled into a dead, dried bud, nothing but a memory. What kind of life would that be? They would be existing in the same space but desiring

61

nothing more than to be as far from each other as possible.

Option one will hurt for days, maybe weeks, while option two will be a constant needle to the heart, a stabbing pain that could never be relieved. She rubs her heart, already feeling the ache.

"Leave him," she says out loud, one eye closed. She dreads what is going to appear before her. The next few minutes will plot out her life for a period of time. She has done this so many times she has lost count. She wishes the worrying suspense would cease to exist but every time, it leaves her shaking in anticipation.

Her life used to be routine. It used to be one that she could predict. She got up, went to work, came home, read, made dinner, watched TV, and went to bed. That was the general script, only occasionally disrupted by something such as vacation or a defining life moment like a birthday or marriage. In general, however, the world she lived in was comfortable and simple.

Then this damn book showed up on her doorstep, and she stepped from the mundane into the seemingly extraordinary.

At first it had been exciting, saying the choices out loud and watching her life laid out for her. It took out the hard decisions and constant worrying. She knew what was coming, no surprises.

To her it sounded fabulous. A life where she could just drift on only having to think hard occasionally. It sounded great until she watched her life and dreams begin to fail before her eyes. The words spell out fate and there isn't a damn thing she could do about it.

She knew how she was going to be fired before her boss ever rose his voice. Knew her beloved dog was going to get hit by a car before he ever dashed out into that street. Knew her parents were going to call and tell her they were moving, before the phone ever rang. She had tried everything to avoid those moments but all paths led to the same fate, no matter where she tried to run. It was like she was in a maze. Every time she tried to make a different turn, she would hit a dead end, forcing her back. Each move she made pushed her toward the end the book wanted. Since she had opened the spine and read out that first choice, her life was no longer her own.

She holds her breath as the words appear. A minute later, they had stopped. She raises the book to her eyes and begins to read.

You watch as confusion is replaced by despair in his eyes. His face sinks and he reaches out a hand for yours. You don't let him touch you, knowing contact will only make this that much more difficult.

"I'm sorry," you tell him, lying your key on the counter. "I love you, but I can't be a part of this anymore. I don't know who I am, where I'm going." You hold his gaze. You don't cry, don't have a cracking voice. To an outsider, you look and sound cold and soulless.

"But we can work on that. I don't even know what happened." He is reaching out for you, grasping at the air, his mouth working like a fish out of water. He needs details and reasons. He needs you to make him understand.

You know you can't. You walk around the counter, kiss his cheek, and walk out of the room. You aren't surprised when he chases you, grabbing your arm. He pulls you to face him, eyes begging for a better explanation than what you have already given him.

You don't say a word, just pry your fingers loose and leave the house. His saddened eyes watch you through the glass as you back out of the driveway and away from him.

You ignore his calls, emails, and text messages. Severing all ties is what will make each day a tiny bit more bearable. Holding on, even with just a finger, only complicates the whole ordeal. He'll move on and heal, as he always has done before.

Two months later you get the call. He has hit a tree with his car, whether it is an accident or deliberate is unknown. He lies in a coma, and chances of him waking up are slim.

She falls against the wall, hand over her mouth. She feels the tears soaking her cheeks. Her vision blurs, the words becoming nothing but black slashes.

"No," she whispers to herself over and over again. "No, please, no."

The book is open to the last words on the floor beside her. She has no idea how long she sits on the ground sobbing about losing a love and friend she hasn't actually lost yet. The door opens and closes, the sound of footsteps brings her back to herself.

"Phillip?" she calls. She can't hide the sorrow or tears. He sees her curled in a ball on the ground and is instantly at her side. She claws at his chest and snuggles in close.

"Shhh…" he whispers to her. "What happened? Your mom? Dad? Brother? Sister? Becca? Teri?" He keeps rattling off names. She knows he is waiting for a screech of pain that will signal that he has found the right person. The sound will never come.

Once he runs out of names he goes silent, just letting her sob into his side. Her sobs subside to sniffles and he lifts her and places her on the couch. He leaves for a moment. She waits, her heartbeat still pounding in her chest. He turns and hands her a glass of water which she takes with trembling hands."

"I'm sorry," she whispers. He just stares at her, confused. She knows he has no idea what she could have done to elicit this type of reaction.

"For what?" His words are gentle but hesitant. She knows he is holding his breath waiting for the one word that will be like a slash across his chest drawing beads of red. Cheated.

"For taking it into my house. For opening it. For not burning it when I had the chance. For letting it destroy us and you." She knew she was making little sense.

She knew he was lost trying to put her words into some type of order.

"Huh?" he finally says. She gets up from the couch and goes into the kitchen. It was still sitting on the floor, the last pages glaring up at her. She picks it up and shuts it. Its smooth surface slicked with tears.

Shaking, she walks back into the living room and hands him the book. He takes it, confusion starting to give him a headache. What was this?

"A book is destroying us? How?" She flips it open to the last page she had been on and let him read it. Confusion evaporates replaced by understanding and then panic, an all-consuming panic.

64

She watches him sink into himself. His hands shake and his mouth hangs open. She expects him to look up and tell her they will figure something out, not for him to practically rip the pages from the binding to reach the last page.

She had settled from her initial shock and panic. Now she felt the fingers of that panic taking hold again. What happened? What had he'd seen that she had missed?

He reaches his destination and drops his head into his arms. She doesn't hear anything but judging by the way his shoulders rise and fall he was the one crying now. She reaches out and grasps his shoulder.

"Phillip?" she whispers "What's wrong?"

He looks up, eyes red and face tear-stained. He holds open the last page to her and she takes it into her hands.

She has never flipped to this final page before; she has always been concerned only by what was immediately before her.

Written on the top of the last page were two choices and a few paragraphs.

Reveal the book.

Keep it a secret.

She feels her breath catch in her throat. Below them it read, *Reveal the Book.*

You tell him the book's secrets. He sees how it works and a sudden realization hits him. It was only supposed to be a prototype. No civilian was supposed to ever see the pages. There were too many bugs, too many variables. He had told them it was too dangerous. Told them all the books needed to be destroyed. Why had this one not been burned like all the others? Why was it back to haunt him? Who would do this to him?

You have told him about the book, shown it to the world. That was not allowed, ever. There was a safety measure incorporated into the book as a precaution. The idea was to eliminate the source of the knowledge, if they did not breathe the secret would remain safe. It was also meant to shock and scare the one who they told. Watching the demise of the one who shared the secret should be enough to scare them into silence. The idea was to keep the secret as long as possible.

You look into his eyes, vision going fuzzy as the world recedes away from you. You get to say one last, "I love you," before your heart

65

stops and you brain turns off.

She looks up and finds his gaze. His eyes beg for forgiveness. "It was my fault. I shouldn't have let this happen. I'm sorry." She nods instantly forgiving him. She has no idea what he is apologizing for but she does not have the luxury of time to get anymore answers, answers that do not mean anything anymore.

A sense of calm steals over her, "I love you," she whispers as she feels the light fading. It happens in a single second. One moment they are watching each other; the next, it is only his eyes that can still see.

The book slips from her hand, the last page still face up.

Two words on the bottom of the final page say:

THE END.

Enjoyed the stories? Enjoyed being whisked away to another world that is familiar yet a bit unsettling? If you enjoyed these stories be sure to sign up for my mailing list (http://eepurl.com/bwPakf) in order to be the the first to know when I publish something new! Thanks!

Be sure to follow my social media links and blog to stay up to date on the projects I am working on.

Twitter - @shmibby88
Facebook - https://www.facebook.com/BrittneyRz
Blog- BrittneyRz.com
Also find me on Goodreads!

ACKNOLWEDGMENTS:

This book would never have come together if it had not been for the support and encouragement from my family and friends. Thank you to all of you who supported me throughout this entire process.

Also a special thank you to my beta readers. Thank you to my mother, brother, Danny, Aunt Michelle, Uncle Steven and Aleece, for spending time reading over the stories and offering your opinions and ideas. I sincerely appreciate you taking the time to help me make these stories the strongest they could be.

Also thank you to the other members of the writing group, The Lakewood Literary Club, I have been apart of. Your thoughts and comments were greatly appreciated.

ABOUT THE AUTHOR:

Brittney Rzucidlo currently lives in Cleveland, Ohio. She is a graduate (2011) of Miami University of Ohio where she earned a bachelors degree in Creative Writing. She loves to spend her free time reading fantasy and science fiction novels and short stories as well as spending time with her family and friends.

In her spare time she also runs a blog (brittneyrz.com) where she reviews some of her favorite books and tv shows.